THE
VERY BEST
CHRISTMAS TREE

THE
VERY BEST
CHRISTMAS TREE

B. A. King

WOOD ENGRAVINGS BY MICHAEL McCURDY

DAVID R. GODINE * PUBLISHER * BOSTON

First trade edition published in 1984 by
David R. Godine, Publisher, Inc.
306 Dartmouth Street
Boston, Massachusetts 02116

Text copyright © 1983 by B. A. King
Illustrations copyright © 1983 by Michael McCurdy

Library of Congress Cataloging in Publication Data

King, B. A. (B. Anthony)
    The very best Christmas tree.

    Summary: Mr. Bones prefers a very large Christmas tree
and Mrs. Bones prefers a very small one, but together they
pick out the best Christmas tree ever.
    [1. Christmas trees—Fiction. 2. Christmas—Fiction]
I. McCurdy, Michael, ill. II. Title.
PZ7. K572Be 1984   [E]   84-47656
ISBN 0-87923-539-x

I acknowledge gratefully the help I have had with this manuscript
from Deborah McCurdy and Aija Russell.

First edition
Printed in the United States of America

THE
VERY BEST
CHRISTMAS TREE

This story is dedicated to Mrs. Bones
with gratitude and love.

THE BONES FAMILY lived in a funny old house with a front hall that looked as if it had been designed with a big Christmas tree in mind.

The Boneses decorated their tree almost entirely with ornaments they made themselves. After Thanksgiving, a card table was set up in the kitchen so the whole family could take turns making decorations before breakfast, dinner, and bedtime.

Every year there were more and more beautiful

THE BONES FAMILY lived in a funny old
house with a front hall that looked as if
it had been designed with a big Christmas tree in
mind.

When the children were small, Mr. Bones started bringing the Christmas tree home as a surprise. On the first snowy day in December, he would drive to the Southwick Farm in Leicester, Massachusetts, and climb into the battered truck with Farmer Southwick. With the Southwicks' old dog running alongside, they would drive out the farm road behind the barn, through the

ravine by the pond, past the woods where the laurel grows, and up to the high meadow where the tallest evergreens stand.

Each year as they tied the tree to the roof of Mr. Bones's car, Farmer Southwick said, "Be careful you don't bust a gut."

The Boneses decorated their tree almost entirely with ornaments they made themselves. After Thanksgiving, a card table was set up in the kitchen so the whole family could take turns making decorations before breakfast, dinner, and bedtime.

Every year there were more and more beautiful

handmade ornaments, which gave Mr. Bones an excuse to buy a bigger tree than they'd had the year before.

At last the tree was so large that guests had to enter the house through the back door. To climb the front stairs, they had to hug the wall. The little girl whose bedroom was on the third floor could see the top of the tree without getting out of bed.

Each year after the tree was decorated, Mr. Bones would exclaim, "This is definitely the most beautiful tree we've ever had!" And everyone would agree.

One Christmas Mr. Bones noticed that Mrs. Bones was very quiet. He asked if something was wrong. She looked a bit sad and said she wished their friends didn't have to come into the house through the kitchen, and that she was afraid of what might happen if such a big tree caught fire. Mr. Bones promised to buy a smaller tree next year.

But when the time came, the tree he bought was almost as big as the last one. He explained that it had looked smaller before they cut it down. When Mrs. Bones saw it, she sat on the bottom stair and cried. This made Mr. Bones feel like crying too. He promised she could have any tree she liked next Christmas.

Early next December, Mrs. Bones called Mr. Bones at work and asked him to pick up a tree she had chosen. The tree cost twice as much as one of Mr. Southwick's, and the sales attendant smelled of stale beer. The snow around the edge of the vacant city lot looked grimy, and Mr. Bones thought of Mr. Southwick's old dog running beside the truck through the clean snow. When he tied the tree to the car, there was certainly no need for anyone to warn him about busting a gut.

Mrs. Bones's tree was small enough so that it could be set up in the middle of the front hall. It looked lovely, in its own way. Fat and even all around. But it couldn't hold all the homemade decorations and was only big enough for one string of colorful wooden beads. And because the tree had been cut early for its long trip to the city, many of its needles had fallen by Christmas Day.

The children told Mr. Bones when no one else could hear that they liked Mummy's tree okay, but they hoped he would be the one to pick out the tree next Christmas.

Mr. Bones had a better idea. That very day he made a date with Mrs. Bones to go to the South-wick Farm on the first day it snowed the following December to pick out the tree together.

And that is what happened. On the first snowy day in December, Mr. and Mrs. Bones visited Farmer Southwick. They climbed in the truck and drove out the farm road behind the barn, through the ravine by the pond, past the woods where the laurel grows, and up to the high meadow where the tallest evergreens stand, while the old dog ran alongside through the fresh snow.

They picked out a tree, perhaps smaller than
Mr. Bones would have preferred and perhaps
larger than the one Mrs. Bones would have chosen,
but it was a beautiful tree. The children cheered
when they saw it. The tree held all the beloved
ornaments and all three strings of colorful wooden
beads, and friends could still squeeze in by the
front door.

Although the little girl whose bedroom was on
the third floor couldn't see the tree without
getting out of bed, she could smell it first thing
in the morning when she woke because it was so
freshly cut.

Everyone agreed it was the most beautiful tree they had ever had.

This book was set in Linotype Palatino, a typeface designed by Hermann Zapf. Named after Giovanbattista Palatino, a Renaissance writing master, Palatino was the first of Zapf's typefaces to be introduced to America. The designs were made in 1948; the fonts for the complete face were issued between 1950 and 1952.

* * *

This book was designed, illustrated, and typeset by Michael McCurdy. Printed by Daamen, Inc., in Rutland, Vermont, on Monadnock Natural Laid, the book was bound by A. Horowitz & Sons, Fairfield, New Jersey.

* * *